For a TOP SECRET editor and our TOP SECRET Christmas mission – M.S.

For my pie-eating parents and their MAGICAL little sweet shop – S.C.

SANTA'S
WORKSHOP

BLOOMSBURY CHILDREN'S BOOKS
Bloomsbury Publishing Plc
50 Bedford Square, London, WC1B 3DP, UK
BLOOMSBURY, BLOOMSBURY CHILDREN'S BOOKS and the Diana logo are trademarks of Bloomsbury Publishing Plc
First published in Great Britain by Bloomsbury Publishing Plc

Text copyright © Mark Sperring 2018
Illustrations copyright © Sophie Corrigan 2018

Mark Sperring and Sophie Corrigan have asserted their rights under the Copyright, Designs and Patents Act, 1988,
to be identified as the Author and Illustrator of this work

A catalogue record for this book is available from the British Library

ISBN 978 1 4088 9347 0 (HB)
ISBN 978 1 4088 9346 3 (PB)
ISBN 978 1 4088 9348 7 (eBook)

1 3 5 7 9 10 8 6 4 2

Printed and bound in China by Leo Paper Product Ltd, HeShan
All papers used by Bloomsbury Publishing Plc are natural, recyclable products from wood grown in well managed forests.
The manufacturing processes conform to the environmental regulations of the country of origin.

To find out more about our authors and books visit www.bloomsbury.com and sign up for our newsletters

MINCE SPIES

Mark SPERRING ✳ Sophie CORRIGAN

BLOOMSBURY
CHILDREN'S BOOKS

LONDON OXFORD NEW YORK NEW DELHI SYDNEY

In a great BIG supermarket,
not far from your front door,
Christmas treats are FALLING . . .

ARGH!

And CRASHING
to the floor!

Sweet biscuit men lie
BROKEN
and plum puddings have gone

SPLAT!

Candy canes are all in

PIECES,

Christmas cakes
are feeling
FLAT!

And though more get delivered,
the outcome is the same –
a ruined heap of Christmas treats . . .

but **WHO** or **WHAT'S** to BLAME?

Now, luckily for ALL OF US,
someone's planned a BIG surprise –
a secret YULETIDE mission
for the CRIME-FIGHTING

MINCE SPIES!

So, with FLAKY PASTRY jetpacks,
they've all flown into town . . .

And their TOP SECRET MISSION is to track the VILLAINS down.

But as the hours tick by . . .

there's NO hint of any CRIME.

Then a WALKIE-TALKIE springs to life . . .

ALL AGENTS TO AISLE NINE!

In one super-speedy second –

WHOOOOO

– the Mince Spies get to work,

SH!

grabbing extra-cheesy breadsticks
and whipped cream cans to squirt.

They **ZOOOOOOO**
along their ZIP WIRES, high above

OOOM

the dim-lit store . . .

Then **LEAP** towards their TARGET,

With DEADLY little fingers PRIMED on

SPRAY CANS fit to burst,

And, as shadows SPIN across the wall,

OH, HELP!

WHAT WILL THEY FIND?

Perhaps a

SUPER VILLAIN

who has lost his

EVIL MIND!

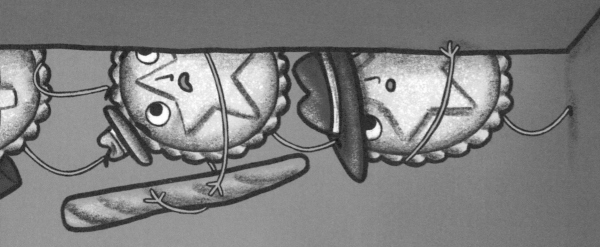

But there CAUGHT
chocolate-handed is . . .

a **GANG** of **SPROUTS**,
no less,

about to send some Christmas logs
HURTLING to their deaths!

wow!

"You CAN'T catch us!"

the Sprouts all squeal.

"So PLEASE

don't

EVEN

try!"

Then off they SCOOT, down aisle nine,
as jets of WHIPPED CREAM fly.

In one SLIP-SLIDEY moment –

KA-SPLODGE!

– things become a STICKY mess.

And Christmas as we know it is in

SERIOUS

DISTRESS!

Whippy CREAM

BEANS

"Send your VERY BESTEST back-up!"
calls a Mince Spy down the phone.
"We need FESTIVE reinforcements,
we CAN'T catch them on our own!"

Then with a JINGLING
of sleigh bells

HO!
HO!
HO!

TWO BOOTS APPEAR.

"We've got you now!" the Mince Spies shout. "LOOK . . ."

"SANTA CLAUS is HERE!"

"Now," says Santa gently, "tell me, what's all THIS about?

How did you turn into a bunch of TREAT-DESTROYING sprouts?"

"Well, it's just that EVERY Christmas," a sprout starts to confess,
"everybody seems to like those sugared SWEET TREATS best.

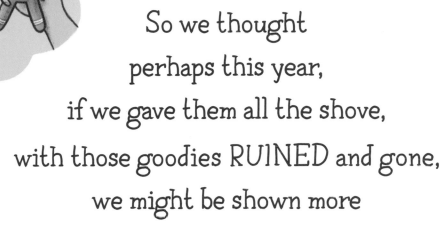

So we thought
perhaps this year,
if we gave them all the shove,
with those goodies RUINED and gone,
we might be shown more
LOVE!"

Santa gave a hearty chuckle,
"Oh, how SILLY you have been,
for you are LOVED
MORE than you know . . .

you're Santa's
FAVOURITE
GREENS!

And, as for acting mean and pushy,
may I offer some advice –
people are sure to LOVE you more
if you are GOOD and NICE!

So give those chocolate logs a HUG
and mend your wicked ways.

Let's fill the shelves with **JOY** and **LOVE**,
it's ALMOST . . ."